T0132248

Flash's Day at the Circus

Charlie Alexander

Flash's Day at the Circus

Written by Charlie Alexander
Artwork by Charlie Alexander

Flash met some friends.

They were boarding the train to the circus too!

Flash helped stroll the twins.

Mary and Sarah enjoyed the ride.

Mathew and Stephanie followed Flash.

Everyone was anxious to see the circus tent!

Flash entered the tent.

He was happy about his special day at the Circus.

The first cow was very surprised to see Flash!

His face had a look of shock!

Flash thought this clown was teasing all the kids.

But everybody liked the way he made them laugh.

The Ring Master announced the show was about to begin.

He looked cool in his hat and suit.

The weight lifter came out first.

He was very strong.

Another strong man was next.

He could lift the two big weights at the same time.

Flash had to show off his skills as well.

He thought he was part of the show!

Flash was a little nervous about this clown.

He found him to be a bit scary!

Flash had a blast on the trapeze.

He imagined catching himself.

Flash rode the elephant.

He arrived but he was facing backward.

Flash and the elephant entered the tent.

By now Flash was standing up and riding on top!

This cow was named Muriel.

She could ride the unicycle like no one else!

Mr. monkey laughed when he watched Muriel.

He knew it was hard to keep her balance.

This clown loved ice cream.

So did Flash.

Flash tried to be in every act.

He just loved the circus. And dressing
in feathers was awesome!

The little piggy was so cute.

Flash made friends with him in a moment!

Flash went to buy a cold drink.

He met a cow on the way.

Flash made it just in time for the tight rope.

It looked difficult not to fall!

The audience applauded when they saw a Giraffe.

Flash was trying to give him a treat.

The seal was a beautiful blue.

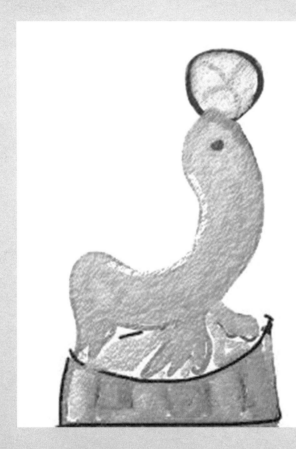

He could balance a ball on his nose!

This clown seemed very sad.

He found out there was no popcorn left.

Flash was a happy clown.

After all, he had two cool balloons.

All the clowns came out together.

What a wonderful show!

Flash laughed out loud.

He had never been on an elephant balancing on a ball!

Be careful Flash!

He was now part of the circus. The horse liked the
way Flash could hold on!.

Another elephant was enjoying a break.

He had a chance to eat some peanuts!

Flash thought he made a great lion.

He just couldn't roar!

This elephant was Flash's friend.

They planned on having lunch together.

The zebra gave Flash an exciting ride.

Flash was careful to hold on tight.

The day went by so quickly.

Fireworks lit up the sky!

The train waited to be boarded by all.

It was time to head home.

Flash loved his day at the circus!

Everyone had the best time!

The End

To order additional copies of this book, contact:
Xlibris
844-714-8691
www.Xlibris.com
Orders@Xlibris.com

ISBN: Softcover   978-1-6698-7692-2
            Hardcover   978-1-6698-7693-9
            EBook   978-1-6698-7691-5

Library of Congress Control Number: 2023908681

Print information available on the last page

Rev. date: 05/09/2023

Printed in the United States
by Baker & Taylor Publisher Services